Tales of Magic and Transformation

Book Two

Haven Island

Camilla Leon

Cover art by Andrew Plant

Dedication:

Much gratitude to Angie Anderson
for her assistance with the publishing of this book.

Published in 2022 by Cassiel Books
Copyright © Diana Hadlow 2022
Cover art © Andrew Plant
Illustrations: Chapter Title Medallion, Chameleon p.44, & Dragon p.52 © Andrew Plant
ISBN 978-1-912484-95-9

Chapter One

Our story begins on Haven Island, one in a group of remote volcanic islands in the middle of a vast ocean. The volcano on Haven Island is long extinct, and the mountains that form the backbone of the island are covered with trees, except for the peaks, which are bare and often snowbound in winter. Below the tree line are valleys with lush green meadows full of flowers, watered by underground springs which fill the rivers and lakes in the lowlands.

Haven Island is ruled by a dragon, and today the palace of King Dragon is in uproar. Tomorrow, his only son and heir celebrates his 14th birthday and coming-of-age ceremony, but the prince is missing from the palace and has not been seen for two days. In a fury, the king summons the prince's bodyguards.

'Where is my son?' he bellows. 'It's your job to guard him, so WHERE IS HE?' The two warthogs quake with fear. 'If he is not here tonight, I'll roast you both alive!'

A burst of flames shoots forth from the king's massive jaws, just short of the guards. 'Find him NOW!'

The guards race towards the forest, only stopping when they find a safe place, hiding out in an empty den in order to catch their breath. The king employed them because they looked strong and fierce, but despite their appearance, the warthogs loved their own families and offspring dearly, and were secretly appalled at the way the king treated his only son.

'Where d'you think he's gone?' asked Hogswill, the fatter of the two. 'I told you we shouldn't let him go roaming by himself.'

'He's very clever at slipping away whenever we're on our rest breaks,' said Walter, the smaller guard.

'Yes, but you know we're meant to take separate breaks.' There are a few moments of guilty silence, then Hogswill continues: 'The trouble is, I feel sorry for him. He has no fun, does he? What with all his royal duties... even when he isn't working, the king is always criticising and making the poor little fella's life hell.'

'It doesn't surprise me he's gone,' said Walter, 'And his father is always complaining that he isn't a real dragon. What can you expect? With a toad for a mother and a father who's a dragon, it's no wonder he looks, well... different.'

'True,' agrees Hogswill. 'I bet he's done a runner, before he has to swear to become king after old Dragon-fire falls off his perch. It's obvious he hates all the royal hoo-hah.'

'Yeah, but where is he now? He can't fly like his dad.' Walter shakes his head from side to side. 'Tell you what, there's no way I'm going back to the palace. I don't fancy becoming roast pork. What do you say we go home to our clan in the forest? Nobody will find us there.'

'Good idea,' agreed Hogswill. 'Time to disappear!'

Meanwhile, King Dragon is stomping up and down in the palace stateroom, grinding his great teeth and spurting flames of frustration from his nostrils. Who could have stolen the prince away? The queen? Was the prince with her? Maybe she wants to see him before his "big day". But he quickly rejects this idea. The queen never really wanted children, and her maternal instincts are definitely not one of her strengths.

Their marriage was a formality only, in order to bring peace to the island. When subsequently she realised they needed an heir she reluctantly agreed to have just the one child. But when the child was born the queen thought he looked so ugly she immediately disowned him, saying she wanted nothing to do with his upbringing.

The prince looked like neither of his parents, but had characteristics from both of them. He wasn't as big as a dragon but he was much bigger than a toad. He was certainly different, and some could say he was quite handsome in his own unique way.

However, the king was embarrassed by his son's strange appearance. So to save face and keep his dignity, the king claimed that he and the queen had created a new species, the only one of its kind. At the announcement of his son's birth the king called him a "chameleon". According to his advisors, this meant "lion on the ground" which he decided was a suitably grand title for his heir.

Having eliminated the queen as a suspect, the king wondered who else might want to sabotage the coming-of-age ceremony. Reluctantly, he conceded that the dragons - his own clan - were likely the prime suspects.

Their motive stemmed from the succession of humiliations this proud and powerful race had experienced over the last century.

First, their ancient citadel had collapsed into the sea when the volcano it was built on erupted. Their leader, the Great Lord Dragonus 14th, was forced to request sanctuary on Haven Island, which King Toad had granted.

Then, after a few years, the dragons were banished from the lowlands after some young dragons set fire to a forest. They detested the restrictions, but a Treaty of Territories was enforced in law when the eldest son of Lord Dragonus married the eldest daughter of King Toad. No dragons attended the marriage ceremony. They regarded it as a fiasco, and deeply humiliating for their clan.

It was not surprising, then, that the dragons might want to sabotage the prince's Coming-of-Age and Oath of Succession ceremony, for the signing of that oath would mean one day a half-toad would rule the dragons. One humiliation too many!

But the king knew there was another, more personal motive to betray him and abduct the prince. It all stemmed from the elephant hunt seven years ago, when Lord Dragonus 14th was killed. The clan believed that King Dragon had abandoned them—something they would never forgive.

Chapter Two

Seven years earlier…

The king always loved hunting and regularly joined his father, Dragonus 14th, and his comrades on their hunting trips. He still regarded the prince as a pathetic apology for a dragon, let alone his heir. He needed toughening up, to be prepared for the future when one day he would take over as ruler of Haven Island.

So the king decided to take the seven-year-old prince with him on the elephant hunt, hoping he might see some spark of fire ignited in his son.

The prince had not yet met his grandfather, Lord Dragonus, who controlled his clan through fear, but stories about the dragons' exploits terrified him. He dreaded disappointing his father by refusing to go, but he was quaking with fear. So he pretended to be ill.

The king ignored all the prince's excuses and instead devised a saddle so that the prince could ride on his back. Reluctantly, the prince clambered up and tied himself on for safety. This annoyed the king because it showed his son was scared. They set off, with the prince clinging on tightly as they swooped up into the air, aiming for the mountain peaks. The king roared with delight and the anticipation of the hunt.

They circled over the meeting ground. A huge fire burned below, surrounded by a riotous mass of dragons. It was the pre-hunt bonanza, when the dragons supped strong liquor which fuelled their bellies with fire. Gouts of flame and smoke belched from their jaws as they bellowed their hunting songs. The prince trembled at the sight.

His father landed close to the camp and cheers erupted from the hunting party.

'Better late than never! What kept you?' roared Lord Dragonus.

Lord Dragonus and his generals were impatient to set off. Despite his fear, the boisterous hysteria fostered by the liquor mesmerised the prince. The raging bonfire and the air of rampant anarchy all excited him, and he was further roused by his father's passion.

Three massive dragons dominated the group. Lord Dragonus and his two campaign generals far exceeded the others in size and magnificence with powerful bodies like armoured tanks of muscle and bone. Their scales glinted in the flickering flames of the campfire, and their scythe-like talons, cruel and lethal, twitched under their sheaths, ready for action.

These three were the cruellest of the dragons, and were full of blood-lust and violence, far removed from the more refined behaviour of King Dragon and the diplomacy of his court. In truth, the hunting party only tolerated the king's presence because he was Lord Dragonus's son. In private, they had no respect for him whatsoever.

The comparison between these monstrous muscular machines of power and the weak reptilian form of the prince mortified the king. He quickly regretted bringing the prince and commanded the prince to dismount. Then he hastily removed the riding saddle and hid it behind a rock.

They offered the king a gallon jug of liquor and he slugged it down. The prince lingered near the rocks, too fearful to step forward. The dragons were ripping apart a bear they were roasting over the fire. They didn't care if it was fully cooked or not, they just tore at it with their ragged teeth. The king joined in. Hot oil oozed from the roasted flesh and mixed with fresh blood from the raw meat. It dribbled down the king's jaws—and how he relished its juiciness!

The dragons were in a feeding ecstasy and the noise got louder and louder. Soon the king was drunk like the rest of the clan, and was raring to set out on the hunting trip. Their destination was an island far away to the south where large herds of elephants grazed the pastures. The dragons loved nothing better than swooping down on the herds until they stampeded, terrified by the flame-flowing dragon monsters.

The prince looked for an opportunity to escape this madness and tried to sidle away into a nearby cave. However, the king was looking around for his son and saw him trying to hide. The prince's cowardice disgusted him, so he forced him to climb up on his back, this time without the saddle.

Away they flew, high into the air. Some crazed dragons still carried their gallons of liquor, which spilled over and ignited into flames, cascading through the sky like fiery waterfalls. The prince gripped the scaly ridges of his father's back for dear life. The sheer speed and horrendous cacophony of the dragons turned his fear to terror. He shut his eyes tight and clung on.

The dragons soon spotted the island and zoomed down on it. The elephants were already stampeding with their trunks raised high, trumpeting warning cries. Down swooped the dragons, roaring and blasting flames. They struck out with their lethal claws, not caring that baby elephants were being trampled by the terrified herd. The dragons howled in frenzied excitement. Blood gushed everywhere, saturating the ground which became slippery and treacherous, causing elephants to fall and get injured.

Suddenly, there was an ear-piercing screech, loud even above the terrified screams of the distraught elephants and the blood-curdling dragon cries. From the west, a cloud like a dense black arrow hurtled towards the scene of the massacre. Leading the cloud was the Fury, a bat-winged Goddess, an Avenger of Injustice. She looked grotesque, with blood-red eyes and black robes streaming behind her like inky tentacles. The snakes wrapped around her head were poised, alert, ready for attack.

Flying close to her tail was her loyal battalion of harpies, those monstrous vulture-like beasts who showed no mercy. Their duty was to exact revenge for all victims, taking their orders from the Fury who led them.

The dragons saw their enemies approaching at speed and, like all bullies who are cowards when faced with a stronger force, they quickly changed direction. They flew high, swerving and diving to escape the harpies. The hunters were now the hunted!

The prince, now terrified beyond endurance, fainted and lost hold of his father's scales. Down he fell, tumbling towards the rocks below. The Fury saw his fall and immediately changed direction to fly towards him.

The king watched helplessly as the Fury caught the prince mid-flight. He bellowed out to his fellow dragons for help to rescue his son, but they did not hear him. So it was he alone who flew after the Fury fleeing with her precious hostage. He chased her right into her mountain cavern stronghold, where she turned and confronted the king. He immediately stalled to a halt, flapping his huge wings and hovered before her, in awe of her power.

Inside, the huge cavern was lit by fire torches and her monstrous shadow flickered grotesquely on the cave walls. He recoiled before this goddess who enforced such all-powerful justice. She radiated authority, and he didn't dare look at her engorged red eyes for fear of her judgement. The limp body of the prince still hung perilously, suspended from her massive hooked-wing. The writhing serpents around her head reached down towards the prince, their tongues flickering menacingly.

'Why are you here?' demanded the Fury, her blistering voice echoing around the cavern. 'Dare you plead for your son's deliverance?'

King Dragon was struck dumb with terror.

'Listen well, you petty little king. Your dragons will soon be leaderless, for my harpies even now are hunting your so-called "Great Lord Dragonus". I command **you** to take over his role!' She paused to let her words sink. 'Swear to my conditions, and only then will I release your son.'

Horrified, the king nodded. He still could not speak.

'Now, depart from here! Dragons must never return, or my vengeance will know no end. On pain of death, if you fail me. You **must** control them!' she screeched.

Then she withdrew the winged hook holding the prince, who plummeted towards the ground. The king swooped and caught him in his own claws.

Elsewhere, the harpies, the Fury's wrathful ministers of justice, were focussed on the ringleaders of the hunt: Lord Dragonus and his generals. They did not escape their punishment and they were never seen again. The remaining dragons, many badly wounded, fled back to Haven Island. The king left the harpies' mountain carrying the still unconscious prince. He felt shamed and humiliated, and abandoned by his comrades. Before, he simply disliked his weak son, but now he absolutely hated him.

The Fury had forced the king to take the oath "on the pain of death" if he failed to control the dragons, but he couldn't see how to keep his promise. He was burdened by his royal duties, and he couldn't be in two places at once. As soon as he landed back at the dragon's meeting ground, in desperation he sought his uncle Wotan, the younger brother of Lord Dragonus who had been killed.

Wotan was a peace-loving dragon who repeatedly tried to discourage his brother's cruel hunting trips, but Dragonus had always ignored his advice, calling Wotan a coward and traitor to their proud warrior ancestry. Wotan was deeply saddened by the death of his brother and the pitiful state of the wounded dragons who had returned.

Wotan had already assumed responsibility for taking control of the dragons, and therefore he willingly accepted the formal request by the king to take on the role of their leader. Thus, the king kept his promise to the Fury by delegating the task to his uncle.

The prince remained in a coma for weeks after the hunt. When he eventually regained consciousness he was plagued with nightmares, full of screaming elephants and the shrieks and howls of the Fury and harpies.

His life was made even worse because King Dragon was so angry with his son. 'You realise it was your cowardice that caused this disaster! Had you held on to my back like I said, you would not have fallen and the Fury could not have taken you hostage. Rescuing you meant I had to abandon my father, his generals and the entire clan!'

This was grossly unfair, and the prince learned to blame himself for the gruesome death of his grandfather and other dragons. How he hated himself! How heavy was his burden of guilt!

Chapter Three

The king knew the dragons bore an angry grudge from all those years ago, and suspected they wanted to seek revenge. Desperate to find his son, he sent his army to confront the dragons high in their mountainous lair. The dragon elders denied any knowledge of the prince's whereabouts and were furious to be accused. Still, the army scoured their lairs and caves but found no trace of the prince.

Once the army had left, the younger dragons raged amongst themselves. 'Why didn't we kidnap that disgusting little creature when we had the chance?' one of them hissed.

This renegade band of young dragons had seen the coming-of-age ceremony as their chance to overthrow the king, by capturing his son and threatening to kill him if the king did not surrender his throne to the dragon clan. But three days before their plan was to take place, the prince had disappeared.

'If I find out who leaked our plan, he's dead meat!' roared one dragon.

When the king's army returned, reporting there was no sign of the prince in the dragons' camp, the king was stumped. If not the dragons, who else might want to harm the prince? Who else was there, except the islanders?

The islanders included wild beasts and a variety of forest dwellers living on the wilderness side of the island. But these islanders knew little of royal affairs, so the king quickly discounted them. However, on the more cultivated side of the island, where the town and king's palace and courts were located, lived the merchants and industrious islanders. They were all feverishly active, decorating their stalls in the bustling market-place in preparation for the coming pageant to celebrate the prince's coming-of-age ceremony.

When news of the prince's disappearance leaked out, the traders were dismayed. They were looking forward to increased business from the many islanders who would visit town for the celebrations, but without the prince the ceremony would have to be cancelled. The king quickly deleted them from his list of suspects.

Amid all the chaos searching for the prince, a message was delivered to the king informing him that some beavers had been searching for their adopted son. He had gone missing on the same day as the prince. King Dragon considered this utterly irrelevant until the messenger mentioned the missing son was also a chameleon.

'Also a chameleon! How **dare** you say that!' exploded the king. 'His Royal Highness is unique, the one-and-only chameleon, created by **me**!' (He conveniently forgot the queen had a part in the matter). 'You are a liar! Take him away for execution!' And they dragged the poor messenger screaming from the room.

Chapter Four

Mr and Mrs Beaver lived on the wild side of the island. One day, several years ago, they had found a young chameleon basking in the centre of a huge pink water-lily that was floating on a lake which had mysteriously appeared overnight. They decided to look after him until his parents claimed him. But no parents ever came looking. So they fostered the little creature and called him "Nifty", named for his speed and agility. They already had young beaver kits of their own and happily welcomed the little chameleon into their family.

As Nifty grew older he noticed how different he was to the other animals he met in the forest. Surely there must be others of his kind somewhere? His adopted family were very loving, but as his beaver siblings grew up they started leaving home to create their own families. Nifty could foresee a time when he would one day be alone, and he longed to create a family of his own.

He shared his feelings with one of his best friends, a fairy called Crystalina. 'I love my beaver family, but I want to make a family of my own, yet I've never met another chameleon, let alone a lady one. Do you suppose I'm the only one in the world?' Tears welled in his eyes as he confronted his worst fear, and loneliness overwhelmed him.

Now, it is a fact that the Faerie Kingdom is scattered over all the islands and so the fairies know everything that's going on in their part of the world. To them, it was common knowledge that there was more than one chameleon.

'Cheer up Nifty,' said Crystalina. 'Of course there are other chameleons in the world, although the only one I know of on **this** island is King Dragon's son.'

'Really!' exclaimed Nifty. 'I wonder if we are related?' He paused, his mind re-adjusting to this optimistic news. 'Well, if there is already one chameleon you know about, then perhaps there are others too.'

Crystalina loved Nifty and wanted to encourage his dreams, so she said: 'If it's in your destiny to create a family, Nifty, then you just need to trust that life will take you where you need to go in order to meet your future wife.'

On one memorable day, Nifty was up in the boughs of a tree when he heard a thrashing sound, like the breaking of branches and tearing aside of bushes. Although Crystalina had already told him about the king's son, the sudden appearance of this other chameleon wearing the brilliant colours of the royal dress code shocked Nifty. He remained silent and still, unsure what to expect.

The prince was scowling and muttering to himself as he smashed aside the hanging vines, dislodging frightened birds and monkeys. He kicked out at the rabbits, squashing ant nests, and lunging after the baby deer. He was apparently unaware of the beauty around him as he stomped over rare orchids and delicate wildflowers. Nifty was dismayed, yet could not deny the bond he felt with another creature of his kind.

However, he was disturbed by the anger and cruelty the prince had displayed, so later that evening he went to visit the wise old owl nick-named "Wizzole" and confided in him.

When Wizzole was a young owl he had been an advisor to the king, so he was familiar with all that went on in the palace. But such a privileged role entailed a prohibition from discussing royal matters, and although he knew the prince was a chameleon like Nifty, he'd been unable to speak about it. However, now Nifty had discovered the truth for himself, Wizzole felt free to tell him something about the prince's home life.

'The thing is, Nifty, we learn by imitation. We copy the behaviours of grown-ups around us. Unfortunately for the prince, those around him are cruel, vicious and self-centred, so little wonder he is so aggressive.'

'Is there no hope for him, then?' asked Nifty.

'Of course there is, my dear fellow,' said Wizzole, recognising the disappointment in Nifty's voice. 'Behaviours that have been learnt can be unlearnt. But it isn't always easy to change, so the prince would have to feel it was worth the effort.'

'And what would make that happen?' asked Nifty.

'Maybe look at what the prince has missed out on,' said Wizzole. 'From what I understand, he's not really been allowed to play or have any sort of fun.'

Wizzole paused, choosing his words carefully.

'It might be helpful to know something about the background of the Royal Family. Lord Dragonus forced King Dragon, the prince's father, into an unsuitable marriage with Queen Toad, simply to legalise the dragons' right to live on this island. So the king sees nothing wrong in forcing his own son, the prince, into a role he is unfit for.'

'I see,' said Nifty, 'So he's trapped in his role?'

'Indeed. In public, the king calls his son the "Special One", but it's just a pretence the king hides behind because deep down he feels ashamed that his son is not a proper dragon. In private, the king constantly criticises the prince, and I think the prince believes that neither of his parents love him.'

'Oh, that sounds awful,' said Nifty.

'The only thing the prince seems to believe about himself, simply because his father brags about it so much, is that he's the only one of his kind, the "Special One". And that's why he assumes airs and graces, and is so vain and arrogant.'

'He seemed so angry when I saw him in the forest,' said Nifty.

'Well, his father, King Dragon, is often angry. And the prince has no siblings to play with or learn from. The rules about what he can and cannot do are strict. He has no freedom, no time to play, and no actual idea of what he truly likes. Much of the time he is lonely, with no friends to talk to, only servants.'

'Goodness, no wonder he escapes to the forest,' said Nifty. Something else was bothering Nifty. 'Wizzole, given that the prince and I are both chameleons, how come we are so different?'

Wizzole laughed. 'I'm sure you can answer that yourself. Look at your beaver siblings—are their personalities all alike?'

'Goodness me, no! They are so different that I wonder sometimes where their different characters come from.'

'And why do you think that might be?' asked Wizzole.

After a long pause Nifty replied, 'Well, I suppose it must be something we are born with.'

'That's true, but what if you are not allowed to express yourself? What if right from the beginning of life, you are forced to conform to rules that prevent you even knowing what you are really like?'

'What—you mean like the prince?'

'Exactly!' said Wizzole.

'How dreadful! No wonder he's angry and vicious.' said Nifty.

Wizzole continued with his explanation. 'The prince's "specialness" is on the surface only, placed on him like a label, a bit like the regimental uniform he has to wear. Whereas your feeling of being special comes from deep inside, from the love you were given early in life.'

Nifty remembered with gratitude the many kind things his adopted beaver family had done for him, like building a special entrance to the lodge above the waterline, because chameleons don't like to live in water like beavers do. They respected the fact that he was different from them.

'If you want to get to know the prince, then you need to be very careful and patient. Simply be yourself and encourage him to play. Above all, if he is rude or unkind, don't take offence. It's just the way he has learnt to behave.'

'Thank you, Wizzole. You have given me much to think about. Goodnight.'

'Goodnight, Nifty. Sleep well—although. I won't be sleeping yet. It's time for me to go hunting!'

Then, with a whoosh of his wings, Wizzole flew off and disappeared silently into the forest.

Chapter Five

Although Nifty desperately wanted to meet this other chameleon, he was a bit scared after witnessing how unpredictable and violent the prince could be. So he asked Wizzole's advice once again.

Wizzole called together the community of forest dwellers and told them Nifty wanted to make friends with the prince.

'We all love our dear friend Nifty, but we also know he is different, with no others of his kind to befriend, and he longs to meet another chameleon. I would like to suggest that we, as a community, try to help him.

'There is only one other chameleon I know of, and that's the king's son. According to Crystalina, our contact in the Fairy network, the prince often escapes the restrictions of palace life to wander in our forest. Nifty's plan is to arrange a chance encounter with the prince on one of his forays. Then he will invite him to tea, here with us. We will make the prince feel welcome, show our respect, and foster Nifty's efforts to make friends with the prince. It will also give Nifty protection in case he needs it.'

There was a great hubbub between the members of the community as they shared their ideas and suggestions. Few had any knowledge of the palace or had met any of its residents. They were excited at the prospect of meeting a real prince. A strategy was agreed, with each member contributing.

A few days later, once again, the prince gave his bodyguards the slip and escaped from the palace grounds. He was tramping through the forest when suddenly a chameleon appeared in front of him. He stopped abruptly in his tracks. He couldn't believe what he was seeing. Until this moment he had no idea other chameleons actually existed, for he believed he was special, the only one of his kind.

Nifty was ready to disappear behind his camouflage if necessary and shimmy up the nearest tree. However, he took a deep breath and stepped forward into the prince's path and made a little bow.

'Good morning, Your Excellency.' Nifty lifted his head respectfully. 'What a wonderful honour! I am so delighted to meet another chameleon—especially one of such grandeur and importance.'

The prince gawped. He couldn't believe his eyes.

'My family and I would be honoured if you would have afternoon tea with us,' said Nifty.

The prince was so caught by surprise that he replied automatically to Nifty's formal invitation.

'Yes, yes, that would be most welcome.'

Nifty led them to the edge of the forest where the animals and other islanders were gathered by the river banks, cheering and waving flags.

At first, it didn't look like it would go too well. The prince quickly made it clear that such humble surroundings were beneath his dignity, and that the offered meal of fruits, nuts and leaves was not his usual fare. However, the beaver family did what they could to make the prince feel welcome and honoured. They had made a special herbal tea for the occasion and the prince liked its taste.

Then some islanders presented him with home-made honey and cakes whilst the local band played an off-key rendering of the royal anthem. Soon, the prince felt he was bestowing a great honour and privilege on these lowly creatures. Flattered, and puffed up with self-importance, he showed a condescending display of gratitude.

'Thank you, my island subjects, for honouring my presence. I appreciate your efforts to show due respect to our royal personage.'

He was surprised to discover he had enjoyed the afternoon, so when Nifty asked him to visit again, he agreed.

He did not, however, invite Nifty to visit the palace, for he wanted to keep his royal life secret and protected. The prince knew his father would see Nifty as a threat because he was another chameleon. It would threaten the prince's special, 'only-one-of-a-kind' status. Very likely, the king would want to kill Nifty.

Chapter Six

Over time a friendship developed between the two chameleons. Nifty was keen to understand the prince and his life.

'What made you decide to visit this side of the island?'

The prince was still guarded about revealing too much of his life, so his answer was rather pompous.

'Well, in case you are not aware, my little friend, I am the King Dragon's only son—and the future monarch of this island—so I always have bodyguards to protect me. The problem is they follow me everywhere, and that limits my freedom. Sometimes I manage to slip away and escape into the forest, but only when they go for their lunch break.'

'Have you never tried to camouflage yourself?' asked Nifty.

The prince looked puzzled, not understanding the word camouflage.

'What I mean is, have you ever changed your appearance? Changed your colours, so that you become invisible?'

Nifty demonstrated his words by immediately disappearing, assuming a range of colours and patterns on his skin that blended into the background, making it almost impossible to see him.

The prince was flabbergasted. He had been taught to display only his regimental colours. He had no idea that such camouflaging was possible, and certainly had no clue how to do it. It irritated him that his scruffy little chameleon friend could play around so freely, changing his appearance with such amazing skill. Yet, despite himself, he was fascinated by Nifty's ability. So he asked him to do it again… and again… and again!

Nifty taught the prince how to play hide-and-seek. Playing was a novel experience for the prince. Nifty knew he had to be careful because the only play the dragon clan knew was the hunt! But Nifty was fast. He would disappear, then quickly reappear if he felt the prince was getting too frustrated trying to find him. He didn't want to anger the prince, he just wanted him to have some fun.

One day, after disappearing and reappearing a few times, Nifty said to the prince: 'You know, you could do this too if you wanted to. Your bodyguards wouldn't be able to see you if you weren't so easily spotted displaying your regimental colours.'

The prince instantly responded without thinking: 'But as the king's heir I am duty bound to display my regimental colours at all times! My father would be furious. No, no, I couldn't possibly do that!'

But then the thought of giving his bodyguards the slip by disguising himself was a tempting idea indeed. 'Well, perhaps I could give it a try.'

The prince convinced himself that if Nifty, who was only a common chameleon, could do it, then he would be able to do it even better.

So Nifty showed him how to adjust the colours of his special skin cells which lay just underneath his scales. To the prince's delight he instantly noticed slight colour changes. He was so excited he doubled his effort and before long he was changing his colours almost as quickly as Nifty.

The prince grew to really like Nifty. This was his first ever friend. Spending more time with Nifty influenced his moods and gradually caused him to change. He wasn't so cranky, and he was noticeably less irritable with his bodyguards and less rude to his servants. The king was notified of these changes in his son, and was pleased. He believed his son might finally be taking his role of 'king-in-waiting' seriously. But the king was mistaken.

As his fourteenth birthday approached the prince became increasing depressed. The prospect of taking an oath and committing himself to becoming the next king felt more and more like a future of bondage to duty and responsibility. He felt trapped, like a slave bound forever to act out a role he despised. When he took that oath, any chance of freedom would be lost forever. He began to dream of running away, escaping to the forest and never going back to the palace. He fantasised about becoming skilled in the art of camouflage. It could be just what he needed to set himself free.

Chapter Seven

Meanwhile, all the news about the upcoming ceremonies when the prince would take the Oath of Succession galvanised the young dragons into action. Ever since their arrival on Haven Island, they'd experienced one humiliation after another. Losing their homeland, together with the shame of needing to take sanctuary on an island ruled by a toad, was a loss of face they could not forget. It was still a deep wound eating away at their pride.

Their resentment intensified further when the Treaty on Territories restricted their freedom to roam the island. This was then followed by the indignity of Lord Dragonus's eldest son being married off to the toad king's daughter, simply to ratify an agreement!

On the day of the elephant hunt when they saw King Dragon flying away and deserting them in the midst of the battle, whilst Lord Dragonus and his generals were massacred by the harpies, they were outraged. The remnants of this once proud clan were now permanently demoralised and each bore a deep grudge.

They never forgave the king for abandoning them. So they waited until the younger dragons matured into a formidable clan of fighters, when they'd be ready to take revenge on the king.

The coming-of-age ceremony presented that opportunity. They would never allow themselves to be ruled by such a pathetic half-breed. They made a plan to capture the prince right in front of the crowds during the middle of the ceremony. It would be a magnificent public humiliation of King Dragon, who had betrayed their clan. Then they would announce that they would choose a new king — a younger dragon from their own clan who would rule the island. They knew the palace bodyguards were cowards, and the islanders were not strong enough to challenge them.

It wasn't long before Crystalina heard an ugly rumour through the Faerie Kingdom grapevine that a group of young dragons were plotting to kidnap the prince and take over as rulers of the island. Details of the plot and its timing were unclear, but it was obvious this did not bode well for the islanders.

She told Nifty to warn the prince. It shocked the prince to learn of the kidnap plan, but he did not believe they could succeed.

'Don't be ridiculous! I have bodyguards watching me all the time, to say nothing of the army of soldiers that protect the palace. There's no way a puny group of dragons could penetrate the palace grounds to abduct me.'

'But what about when you come here, into the forest?' asked Nifty. 'Perhaps it would be wise to tell your father about these rumours.'

'My father would want to know where I heard such a rumour. Or he'd see it as an imaginary threat I concocted and just another sign of weakness in me. And I don't want him to know about my visits to see you. I'll wait until we hear something more definite before I risk telling the king anything.'

Chapter Eight

It was a warm afternoon, and the prince and Nifty took a break from camouflage exercise to stroll down to the beach, only to be surprised to find a strange ship in the bay and a group of pirates on the beach.

The dragons normally kept a look-out for uninvited visitors to the island. They enjoyed their role of policing the island's borders. But on this fateful day they were rehearsing their plot to kidnap the prince, so they did not immediately notice the galleon and its host of treacherous pirates.

Unfortunately, Nifty and the prince walked right into their path.

'Camouflage yourself!' hissed Nifty.

Nifty immediately changed his colours to a speckled beige, the same colour as the sand. But the prince knew nothing about pirates. He thought they were just fellow islanders. He did not know they had been hunting wild boar and rabbits to replenish their dwindling food stores. Even worse, the pirates took pleasure in terrifying the local islanders and had no hesitation in killing anyone who got in their way.

So it was that, being blind to the danger, the prince approached the pirates quite fearlessly. He stepped forward and welcomed the sailors

to the island in his most royal manner as the future King of the Realm, making himself as flamboyant as possible by turning on his royal regimental colours.

Startled, but fascinated by this colourful animal, two pirates immediately grabbed him, shoved him into a sack and threw it into one of their rowing boats on the seashore. Nifty raced down the beach and sneaked into the rowing boat carrying the sack, quickly changing his colours to match the wood of the boat. When the rest of the pirates returned with the spoils of their hunt, they rowed out to the galleon and unloaded their booty. They planned to present the exotic creature they'd captured to their captain, to win his favours and put him in a good mood. They had no idea that Nifty was a stowaway onboard.

Belatedly, the dragons saw the pirate ship and swooped down to attack. But the galleon shot cannon fire at them long enough for the ship to make its escape. The dragons turned back, ignorant of the fact that the prince was on board.

Chapter Nine

When Nifty did not come home for his tea on that unforgettable day, Mrs Beaver was worried sick. Nifty loved his food and never missed a meal so they knew something was wrong. The family organised a search party to look for him, but there was no sign of him anywhere. They didn't know the prince had also disappeared until Crystalina flew by and told them the prince was missing from the palace.

'Well, I feel a little better knowing they've disappeared together,' said Mrs Beaver. 'I bet those two scamps have gone off somewhere playing hide and seek. Do you remember how we laughed about how difficult it is to find someone you can't see? And now Nifty has taught the prince how to camouflage himself, they'll be almost impossible to find.'

'You could be right,' said Mr Beaver. 'But I wish those dragons had never come to this island. They've caused nothing but trouble.'

'Oh, really?' exclaimed Mrs Beaver. 'What about the fact they got rid of those trolls that used to terrorise us at night? And the time they rescued those silly pixies who were stranded up in the mountains? And when they saved the gnomes who got caught out in a storm?

They just plucked them, boat and all, out of the sea and brought them to land. Even better,' she continued, having got into a flow of positive memories of the dragons being helpful, 'Remember when they stopped the forest fire from spreading by using their flames to create a firebreak?'

'Okay, okay. I take your point. They aren't all bad.'

Mrs Beaver sighed. 'Well, I just hope and pray Nifty is alright. I miss him terribly.'

'Me too,' agreed Mr. Beaver. 'But if I know Nifty, he'll keep them both safe. I'm sure he'll let us know what's happening when he can. He'll know we'll be worrying about him.'

Chapter Ten

Once on board the ship, the pirate crew presented their exotic gift to their captain (whose name was Captain Sharkeye). He immediately put the reptile inside a locked cage which he hung from a hook in his cabin. Nifty hid nearby on top of a bookshelf so he could whisper to the prince, and try to calm the prince's fears.

Captain Sharkeye was fascinated by the brightly coloured reptile and fed it scraps of food from his own meal table. However, it was the moths and other insects that Nifty caught which kept the prince alive. Now their roles were reversed, as Nifty had more power than the prince, who felt humiliated by his helplessness.

The prince remained depressed and full of guilt at his stupidity in trusting the pirates and involving Nifty in his folly. He lay prisoner on the bottom of his cage, sighing deeply, whilst tears spilled from his eyes and trickled down his nose. He pined for all he had lost. He'd even forgotten how to camouflage himself and was still stuck in his regimental colours.

One morning, as Nifty gave the prince his breakfast of the various moths and insects he'd caught overnight, he chatted to his friend.

'I'm sure Your Excellency is missing the rare delicacies you used to have for your meals at the palace, but these are the most nourishing fare I can find and it's better than the rubbish the captain tries to feed you.'

The prince looked up at his friend, glum and forlorn.

Nifty felt sorry for the prince. 'We won't always be on this ship. I overheard the captain saying they have set a course for their homeland. If you can re-learn how to camouflage, when we reach land I'm sure there will be opportunities for us to escape, and then we'll both be free.'

Nifty always addressed the prince as "Your Excellency". He didn't know what else to call him. And the prince did not use Nifty's name at all, for he'd only ever commanded servants. But on this particular morning, after being fed the tasty morsels Nifty had given him, the prince said: 'Thank you, Nifty!'

Nifty was surprised.

The prince looked up at Nifty. 'It seems silly hearing you call me "Your Excellency" when I'm stuck powerless in this cage.'

'What would you like me to call you?' asked Nifty.

The prince had never been called anything except "Your Excellency" and had to think awhile.

'How about if I call you "Prince"?' suggested Nifty.

After a pause, the prince smiled and replied, 'Yes, I like that. Not as a title, just a name. Thank you, Nifty!'

Nifty grinned and said, 'You're welcome, Prince.'

Once Prince settled into a routine with Nifty feeding him regularly and chatting to him through his cage, he resumed his camouflage practice. These sessions took place whenever Captain Sharkeye left his cabin. Day after day they worked at it. One day, the captain surprised them by returning earlier than usual. He was shocked when he couldn't see his pet reptile in the cage and he spent some time searching around the floor of his cabin. Yet when he looked up at the cage again, Prince had resumed his normal colouring. Captain Sharkeye assumed he hadn't looked at the cage properly and he must be more drunk than usual... maybe his name should be Captain Fisheye!

Chapter Eleven

Mr Beaver had been right to say he was sure Nifty would let them know what had happened as soon as it was possible. After a few days, a seagull arrived with a message explaining what had happened. The seagull said the information was for the Beaver family alone—a secret the Faerie Kingdom asked them to keep.

When Prince and Nifty sailed away from Haven Island they could not imagine their voyage would last nearly a year.

Nifty missed his beloved beaver family, but instead of moping he used the services of migrating birds to relay messages back to Haven Island, telling his news and sending his love. His family sent return messages full of love and support, which uplifted his spirits.

Weeks dragged on, so to fill the time Nifty and Prince shared their life stories. These tales helped them understand each other better and, for Prince, it was a healing experience. For the first time, he was able to talk about the cruelty and neglect shown by his parents.

With so much time to reflect, Prince became disturbed as memories of past traumas resurfaced in his mind. Nightmares plagued him and he needed to share his burden.

'I'm sorry to stress you with these awful memories, Nifty. Please tell me to stop if you can't bear it.'

'Dear Prince, I'm just so sorry you were treated so badly. If I'd been there I would have tried to help you.'

Prince recalled the terror of the elephant hunt. He knew he needed to open up and share the story of what he'd experienced.

'When we arrived at the meeting ground, I couldn't believe what I was seeing and hearing. The noise of the dragons roaring their hunting songs, with gouts of flame spurting from their jaws. I remember a huge bonfire. They were roasting a bear and they tore it apart with their massive talons. The smell of gory blood and oil from cooked flesh mixed together, and made me feel sick. When my father joined in I saw a side of him which terrified me. He was in a frenzy of rage like the other dragons.'

It took a long time for prince to share this story. The memories came back in fragments.

'I remember falling off the king's back and spinning downwards towards the ground. The next thing I recall, I was hooked onto the wingtip of some monstrous witch and she flew off with me. I was dangling perilously, petrified she would let me fall. My father, the king, followed us to her lair in the mountains. What filled me most with dread was seeing my father so afraid when he faced this creature. He couldn't even look her in the eye or speak!'

'Weeks later, when I regained consciousness, my father said it was all my fault. If I hadn't been taken as a hostage, he could have stayed to protect his father and the other dragons from being butchered by the Harpies. So it's all my fault! I can't bear it!'

Nifty listened attentively as Prince told his horrific story. Prince needed to tell the story several times, each time with new layers of trauma re-surfacing. His heavy load of guilt and gut-wrenching remorse gradually lightened. Nifty showed nothing but a compassion for his friend. Only much later did Nifty gently explain where the blame, guilt and shame really belonged—and that certainly wasn't with Prince.

To take Prince's mind off their situation and distract him from his depression, Nifty talked about his early life. The contrast between their experiences was so extreme that prince came to understand that the loving home Nifty had enjoyed and the sweet generosity of the beavers, who not only took him into their home but made him one of the family, was what made him so gentle and loving now.

Chapter Twelve

When it came to telling his own life story, Nifty was keen to raise the spirits of his caged friend. So he focussed on describing the memories that might uplift and distract his companion.

'My first memory was of waking up inside a pink waterlily, floating on a lake,' he began.

Prince growled. 'Stop right there! I'm not a sick child that you have to amuse with fairy stories, nor a senile old fool who has lost his marbles. So please don't patronise me!'

There was a stunned silence. Nifty didn't know what had suddenly upset his friend, but he would not cower when he knew his own intentions were good.

'I'm sorry if you think that's what I am doing, but I am telling you the truth about my early life. I know it is sounds very different to your own experiences, and it may even sound like I'm telling you fairy stories, but my early life was really quite unusual. I thought you might be interested in hearing about it.'

There was a strained and somewhat embarrassing silence, then Prince replied, 'I'm sorry, Nifty. Sorry to be so grumpy. It's just I can't get my head around how different our lives have been. Please continue.'

Nifty took a deep breath. 'One day I woke up inside a pink waterlily. The sun was shining down on the flower and warming me, and the waterlily was rocking gently as it glided along the current of the lake. I awoke with a wonderful sense of joy at the perfection of everything. Then I realised I was hungry. I didn't know what I could eat. I'd had no parents to teach me.

'At that very moment I saw a mayfly and without a moment's hesitation my tongue flew out of my mouth, and caught the insect. Then I swallowed it.'

'Who were your parents?' asked Prince.

'I really don't know,' replied Nifty. 'It never bothered me to find out.'

'Just after I swallowed the mayfly, the snout of a beaver peered over the edge of the waterlily. That was when I first met Mr Beaver. I can't tell you how relieved I was to be rescued. Mr Beaver and his wife offered to look after me until my parents claimed me. They were so loving and kind—the best parents ever!

'They had seven kits already, so I had friends to play with. Four were born the previous year and were all named after favourite foods. There were two males called Poplar and Birch and two females called Willow and Berry. The three younger ones were Bossy, because he **was** bossy, Bobby, because he swam like a cork, bobbing up and down, and Bruce, simply because Mrs Beaver liked the name.

'Their house, or lodge as it's called, looked like a bundle of twigs on the top of the dam Mr Beaver was building. What worried me was all the entrances were underwater, and I hated getting wet. When I told Mr. Beaver he immediately constructed a concealed entrance above the surface of the water, especially for me. I was so grateful and gave him a hug. It showed me they'd truly welcomed me into their family.

'Inside the Lodge it was very cosy, all lined out with clay. Mr Beaver explained they made it under the waterline to protect them from wild animals, like wolves.'

'Or dragons?' queried Prince.

'Possibly,' replied Nifty, 'although Mr Beaver never mentioned dragons. Every morning Mrs Beaver turfed the kits out of bed to practice their swimming. I would scamper off to the forest and shimmy up a tree to catch insects and find fresh leaves for breakfast. I had to watch out for snakes and birds though, otherwise they might eat me for their breakfast.'

Prince shuddered. He'd never thought about being eaten by another creature.

'After I learnt to be less afraid of the water I joined the kits on their jaunts up and down the river, sitting on the back of Birch, one of the older kits. Birch was a real scamp and sometimes he couldn't resist throwing me off his back — just for fun, mind you! Then he'd dive underwater and come up underneath me. Birch explained he only did it to help me lose my fear of water! It terrified me until I learnt to trust Birch would never let me down.'

As time passed Nifty described more of his early life to Prince, who came to enjoy these stories.

'On trips down the waterways I got to know our closest neighbours, a family of river voles, and some huge toads with ballooning throats who croaked all night long. Sometimes the kits joined me in the forest, gnawing the tree bark or collecting branches for the dam. I'd scuttle up and down the trunks and pelt them with nuts and berries. Then they'd either eat them or jeer at my poor aim.'

Prince chuckled, and Nifty could see these talks were helping his friend see a different side of life.

'Tell me more about your beaver family,' said Prince.

'Well, Mrs Beaver was quite a large lady. Whenever she went out, she wore a ridiculous hat. One day, my beaver siblings and I made a plan to persuade her to stop wearing it. I camouflaged myself to look just like the hat and we hid the real one. Along came Mrs Beaver and plonked me on her head instead of her real hat. All the little beavers were trying not to giggle.

'She was about to leave the lodge, when I stood up on her head and screeched "cock-a-doodle-do!" Mrs Beaver was all a-fluster and the little beavers rolled around on the floor in fits of laughter. Then I jumped down and presented her with her real hat. To everyone's delight she chased me round the kitchen, as I kept changing and disappearing before her eyes. Eventually, seeing the funny side, she joined in the laughter. And threw away her hat!'

Prince loved hearing these stories and roared with laughter at their naughty pranks. As his love for his funny and loyal friend grew, Prince's depression gradually lifted.

Chapter Thirteen

Eventually, the ship docked at the sailors' homeland. Captain Sharkeye took the cage and chameleon home with him. He thought his daughters would like to keep it as a pet. Nifty kept close to Prince by hiding himself in the captain's luggage.

The captain's two girls were fascinated by Prince and enjoyed watching him stare at them from behind his cage wires. But the three dogs and two cats instantly hated him and were jealous he was getting all the attention. They tormented him by barking or trying to claw him through the cage bars. It made Prince go rigid with fear, and he lay motionless at the bottom of his cage, pretending to be dead. All Nifty could do was watch miserably from his hiding place behind a nearby packing case. There was nothing he could do to help.

Fortunately Captain Sharkeye saw what was going on. He realised his pets disliked the recent addition to his menagerie, so he decided to take Prince to the local zoo. He knew they had a large reptile house and might like this new specimen.

They travelled to the zoo in his horse and carriage. Nifty hid behind the captain, who was busy driving. He managed to get close to Prince in his cage.

'Prince?' he whispered. 'I saw the animals trying to scratch you. Are you okay?'

'Yes, Nifty, I'm okay. It was pretty scary, though. I thought I might end up as their dinner.'

'I'm sorry I couldn't help. I was hidden behind some boxes and knew if I came out they would chase me. I'd camouflaged myself, but those dogs have a tremendous sense of smell and were sniffing me out every time I tried to get near you.'

'Well, thanks for trying. I guessed you were somewhere around, but I missed seeing you nearby.'

'The captain told his wife he was taking us to a zoo, but I'm not sure what that is. I'll keep as close to you as I can. It's a lifesaver, being able to blend into the background so easily. I'll latch onto the captain's jacket, so wherever he takes you I can tag along as well. So hopefully, we won't be separated.'

Their whispering ceased when the carriage stopped outside the zoo. It was a noisy place, with screeches and cries from all the different animals. Nifty clung on to the back of the captain's coat-tails as they entered the building. With some clever camouflaging and much agility, Nifty was able to slip inside the enclosure alongside Prince. They found themselves in the company of various other reptiles, including chameleons.

Captain Sharkeye and the zookeeper shook hands, and a deal was made. The zookeeper paid the Captain some money and the two chameleon friends were finally left in peace.

'Am I glad to be with you at last!' said Nifty.

'Not as glad as I am to be with you!' replied Prince. 'I just wish I didn't feel like I'm swaying, like I was still on board the ship!'

Here, at least, Nifty and Prince were together and safe. They had plenty of time now to wonder what was happening on Haven Island.

Chapter Fourteen

Back on Haven Island and after many months of searching, King Dragon had to accept the prince was gone for good.

In despair, he left the lowlands and returned to live in the mountains. Without his son, he no longer wanted to remain as king of Haven Island. He had tried to create a powerful royal dynasty, but in the process he had mistreated his son. He had finally realised that his criticism of the prince had been unfair. Now he bitterly regretted it and blamed himself for his son's disappearance.

But the younger dragons still bore their grudge against King Dragon, and they rejected him and threw him out of their camp. And so it was that desolate and defeated, the lonely king found an empty cave and retreated from the world.

The fate of his nephew saddened his uncle Wotan, so he followed the king to see where he would go. Wotan left him to settle awhile before visiting. The king was relieved that not everyone had rejected him and welcomed Wotan to his lair. They spent much time talking, with Wotan listening to the king's sad story of regrets.

When Wotan departed, he flew straight to the cave where the younger dragons were drinking heavily, celebrating the downfall of

King Dragon whom they blamed for all their misfortunes. Wotan strode into the midst of their gathering and waited for them to notice him, for it was rare indeed that elders intruded into their space. At last they noticed him and fell silent.

'Brother Dragons!' he called in a commanding voice. He paused to ensure he had their full attention. 'We are indeed a proud and powerful race!'

Some of the rowdier dragons responded with cheers, which he immediately quashed with a glare.

'But right now, I am ashamed of you!'

The dragons were shocked into silence. He continued, 'You are ignorant of all the facts, yet have decided nonetheless, to blame King Dragon for all your losses. If anyone is to blame it is our own Lord Dragonus, my brother, who led our ancestors into a wantonly cruel massacre of the elephants, just for fun! And much as I loved my brother, he deserved his punishment by the harpies.'

There were a few noises of dissent, but Wotan ignored them.

'Yes, we have all suffered. But King Dragon has suffered more than most. First, he was forced into a degrading sham of a marriage with a toad, just to secure the Treaty of Territories. Then he lost his father in the Elephant Hunt. And then he lost his son and heir. Has he now also lost his clan? Is this fair for a dragon who simply tried to do his duty?'

He paused, letting the young dragons digest his words. 'It is time you honoured him for the sacrifices he made for us. All he has ever done is fulfil his duty, as commanded by his father, Lord Dragonus, to secure us a home in these mountains.'

There was an awkward silence, then Wotan turned and left the cave. The shocked dragons dispersed, each thinking about Wotan's words.

When the younger dragons learned more of the truth, they made their peace with King Dragon and swore allegiance to him. They officially recognised him as the head of the clan and he assumed the title of "His Excellency Dragonus 15th", and rightful role as his father's eldest son. His uncle Wotan became his personal advisor. Thus, he was once again able to honour the oath he had made to the Fury to lead and control the dragons.

As head of the clan, he wisely recognised the need for change. Haven Island held too many bad memories for his proud species, so he sent out dragon scouts to search for a new home. In time, they discovered an uninhabited mountainous island which was perfectly suited to their needs.

Then on one cold, cloudy night, the dragons left Haven Island, never to return. Queen Toad assumed her rightful role as sovereign ruler of the islanders, and with the departure of the dragons, peace, happiness and prosperity returned to the island.

Chapter Fifteen

All this time, the Faerie Kingdom's network had been busy relaying messages between Nifty and Haven Island, and it was usually Crystalina who delivered their news.

It cheered Nifty to learn of the changes, for it meant he might one day be able to go home to his family. Prince was glad the dragons no longer lived on the island, for Nifty's sake, but he felt no desire to return there himself.

Nifty found it exhilarating to be amongst so many chameleons of all different shapes and colourings. It didn't take long for him to become attracted to one very special lady chameleon—and she obviously felt the same way about Nifty too. His dream of being able to settle down and create a family of his own was finally coming true. It filled his heart with love.

Prince, on the other hand, felt like he was in yet another prison. He longed for freedom and to travel, explore, and have adventures. His deep friendship with Nifty had helped him recognise he had feelings and wishes of his own—needs that had to be met if he was ever to be happy.

And to be honest, he also felt jealous. Some chameleons in his enclosure were bigger and more attractive than him, and no-one gave him any special attention. Even Nifty, his faithful friend for so long, was spending more time with his lady friend than with him. Prince longed to escape. He and Nifty talked about it at length. They both recognised that to be true to themselves, they would each have to go their separate ways.

So Prince told Nifty he planned to escape.

'I can't believe, after all we've been through together, that our lives are taking us in different directions,' said Nifty sadly.

'I know,' replied Prince. 'It breaks my heart to leave you, but it's clear we both need different things. I've learnt from you how important it is to be true to ourselves and that leaves us no option but to honour the new directions life is showing us.'

'Dear Prince, you are dearer to me than any brother I could ever have. If it wasn't for you, I'd still be on Haven Island, nestled in the safe cocoon the beaver family created for me. I certainly wouldn't be here in this zoo where I have met the most beautiful chameleon and the love of my life.'

'I'm amazed how things have turned out,' said Prince 'It's not something we could ever have planned. Knowing you have achieved your dream and you'll have a family of your own makes it easier for me to leave you.'

'Will you keep in touch with me, Prince? I'll want to know all about your adventures.'

'Of course I will, Nifty. You are the best friend I've ever had. If it wasn't for my need to be free and to follow my own destiny, nothing would have separated us. In fact, I'm relying on you to keep our bond of friendship alive. It is like an umbilical cord of love that will sustain me if things get tough.'

They hugged each other and despite the tears that flowed, they knew this was the right decision for both of them.

'Nifty, there is one other thing I need to say to you, and I'll regret it forever if I don't tell you now.'

'What's that?' asked Nifty, looking intrigued.

'You have given me my freedom. It's not leaving the island that has made the difference, but the wisdom, love and compassion that you showed me ever since we met.

'It's these qualities in you that have enabled me to unlock the traumas of my life. Those memories shackled me and made me the cruel, arrogant bully you first met. How on earth you managed to get past all that rubbish and persevere with me until we became close friends, I don't know. But thank you, dear Nifty, from the bottom of my heart. For now I am free to follow my destiny.'

Tears were running down Nifty's face as he watched Prince speak. Prince spoke with such honesty and sincerity that Nifty could hardly believe he was the same angry chameleon he'd first met stumbling through the forest. They hugged each other wordlessly, but tearfully. With everything they'd been through together, never would such a bond be broken.

Chapter Sixteen

Throughout the long voyage Prince had depended on Nifty, who never failed him. It had forced Prince to learn humility. Gone was the arrogant bully of the past. He saw leaving Haven Island as a lucky escape from a life of slavery to his father and a life he'd hated. With growing excitement he looked forward to the day of his freedom and a future full of adventures. Prince and Nifty vowed to keep in touch, using the Faerie Kingdom's network of friendly fairies to carry their messages.

Then they prepared Prince's escape plan. Prince practised his camouflaging every day because he knew the power to seem invisible could save his life. He climbed the tall tree in the enclosure and sat in the boughs to study the surroundings of the zoo. Close by was a village with a railway station and he became fascinated by the steam trains that stopped at the station, picking up passengers, then hurried away over the hills to the next destination. He loved the steam and smoke that billowed out of the chimney, and the sparks and flames that erupted from the boiler.

It reminded him of feelings he'd felt for the dragons on the island—flying free, belching out flames and smoke as they defended the island against invaders. Or rescuing stranded islanders. No, the dragons

weren't all bad. And though he did not have wings, he still had some dragon blood in his veins. And it was this dragon's blood that filled him with a craving to be free.

One evening, when the zoo keeper came to the enclosure to check on the reptiles, Prince adopted his camouflage and slipped out through the open gate and away over the hills towards the town and the railway station. A new exciting adventure was beginning!

Nifty climbed the tall tree and waved goodbye to Prince. He wished him well from the bottom of his heart. Then he scampered back down the tree to his girlfriend waiting below. A new life awaited them too.

Epilogue

After some time Nifty did, in fact, return to Haven Island with Mrs Nifty and their young offspring. His beaver family was overjoyed to welcome them all.

Prince had vowed he would never return to the island. But it is possible, even probable, that over time the bond of love between Nifty and Prince might persuade him to change his mind. It could be that Prince will pay them a visit one day—and maybe even become godfather to Mr and Mrs Nifty's growing family.

And who knows? The island might one day become a haven for Prince, too. Anything is possible!

Lightning Source UK Ltd.
Milton Keynes UK
UKHW05081809022 3
416624UK00003B/277